THE LOCKDOWN CLARINET PLAYER

QUICK TIPS FOR THE SELF-TAUGHT CLARINETTIST

LOUISE LAWRENCE

Uptake publications

CONTENTS

A WizWind inspiration

Uptake publications

Taunton. *TA4 2AR*

DEDICATION

Letters from the attic
Her appendix saved for me
Without her inspiration
Where would Wizwind be?

With grateful thanks to
The Lady Behind The Mask

INTRODUCTION

Why do I squeak? How can I make a better sound? Why do some notes sound weaker than others?

These frequently asked questions and many others are answered in *The Lockdown Clarinet Player*, a useful little book to pop on your music stand and dip into when you pause for breath.

During Lockdown, people have been working on all sorts of interesting projects.

I have been using the time to develop *Wizwind*, a strategy I devised to overcome difficulties in reading music. It is proving hugely successful, and my students are finding it exciting and compelling to be able to choose a tune one week and be playing it the next. I realise *Wizwind* is innovative, so I am using this time to prepare it for publication, a task that has been all consuming over the past few weeks.

Coming up for air, in my own bubble, it occurred to me that many other people working from home may be teaching themselves the Clarinet and could do with a friendly piece of advice here or there. Learning on your own can be a frustrating and lonely experience. This book in no way tries to replicate the comprehensive tutor books and online videos already available. Instead, these pages contain advice on the most common issues you are likely to come across along the way. Hopefully you will find this friendly little book interesting and fun.

Why the pictures? Because we all learn differently. An idea put one way can be baffling, put another can be obvious. I'm a visual learner. If an idea is given to me in picture form, I get it immediately and the message endures. Hopefully, my quirky illustrations will act as a trigger, reminding you of the points taught in the text.

This is the rough order of things:

Nuts and bolts of the Clarinet itself.

How best to set it up.

How to get the best sound:

control of mouth, body and breath.

How to manage the instrument:

control of hands, fingers and tongue.

Accessories:

mouthpiece, reeds, and maintenance.

Trouble-shooting -

the type signalled by squeaks.

….Oh yes and

Back page – at the back of the book.

You may want to read this page first….

Happy playing!

PRELIMINARY NOTE:

Throughout this book, left-handers: just reverse all the left and right directions.

1

INSTRUMENT PURCHASE

A BIT OF SAVVY AVOIDS DISAPPOINTMENT

Instrument Purchase – some thoughts:

It is really advisable to buy from a music shop specialising in woodwind instruments. Why? Because instruments usually come from the factory needing final preparation before re-sale – a job their specialist repairer will do. Your instrument will come with a warranty, and the shop's repairer will sort out technical issues. Non-specialist shops often send instruments away to get the job done – which means involving a third party and a frustrating wait for you.

There are plenty of sparkly new instruments available online, but best to be a bit savvy.

Some manufacturers cut corners in construction and/or use inferior quality materials – this will ultimately affect your progress. My instrument technician friends now refuse to work on cheap quality imports because they cannot be made to play well.

Second-hand instruments can be economic and successful if you can get your purchase to a teacher or repairer first. Let them check it through for you before you commit to payment.

The best scenario is you could find a real gem; the worst is you could buy an instrument needing extensive overhaul or repair before it plays as it should. If you go the second-hand route, it's wisest and best to take advice.

2

REED SET-UP AND ADJUSTMENT
THUMBNAIL

The way you set up your reed is vital: if the reed is not in the correct position it can affect the sound.

Select a reed and suck it three times, each time drawing it from the mouth slowly (like a lollipop stick).

Screw the mouthpiece onto the barrel – it's important to do this first because you can then attach the barrel to the rest of the clarinet without dislodging or damaging the reed.

With the mouthpiece hole facing, hold the barrel with your left hand.

Place the reed on the mouthpiece (lower shiny bit uppermost).

Hold the base of the reed with the left thumb.

With the right hand, adjust the reed so it is in line at the sides with just a thumbnail of black showing at top. Never adjust the reed by pushing the tip.

Thumb nail of black

Slide the ligature over the top of the mouthpiece, being careful not to catch the tip of the reed. Pull the ligature down, making sure you are not obscuring the curve of the shiny section of the reed, otherwise you will restrict its flexibility.

Keep clear

The screws should be facing you. You can then screw them up with your right hand.

(Single screw ligatures just screw at the back on the right. Material ones often have holes in the fabric at the front – just be sure to get the holes absolutely central over the reed).

Screw securely, bottom screw, then top – do not force.

TIP

If your reed is getting thin and worn out you can keep it going for a bit longer by putting it higher on the mouthpiece so that hardly any thumbnail of black is showing. It's a quick fix until you can pop a new one on.

For more information on reeds check **Chapter 22.**

PUTTING THE CLARINET TOGETHER

THE SAFE WAY

Think about this:

There are lots of keys on a Clarinet, it's easy to bend them if you don't do this properly.

Here's a simple way that avoids bending the keys. (NB - if you keep the corks greased then you should not have to force anything together).

Hold the lower joint with the left hand, gently clasping fingers over the two big metal cups at the bottom.

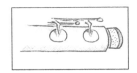

Two big metal cups

With your right hand, twist on the bell.

Transfer the lower joint to the right hand, gently clasping the fingers over those two big metal cups.

Cup the upper joint in the left hand, gently clasping fingers over the open holes and avoiding keys. The four tiny side keys on the upper joint should face you on top.

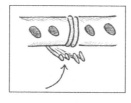

4 tiny keys

Twist the upper joint onto the lower joint, checking the connector keys are in line.

Check Connector keys in line

Now, with bell, lower joint and upper joint all connected together, cup the upper joint in the left hand as before (avoiding the keys), screw on the barrel (NB - mouthpiece with reed should already be attached to the barrel, see **Chapter 2)** and twist it around so that the reed is in line with the single finger hole and thumb rest at the back of the Clarinet.

When you play, the reed will be on your bottom lip.

4

MOUTHPIECE POSITION - EMBOUCHURE
SKIN OF LIP

Skin of lip

Controlling the sound you make is hugely dependent on how much mouthpiece you use and where the reed sits on the lower lip (the embouchure).

Try this:

Place the index finger on your lower lip.

Gently push all the fleshy red section of the lower lip over the lower teeth – *check on how this feels*.

NB: this is too much bottom lip.

Now place the index finger on the lower lip and repeat the exercise, but this time just pushing in *half* the fleshy red section of your lower lip – this feels like just the skin of the bottom lip – *check on how this feels.*

NB: this is correct.

You have already set up the reed on the mouthpiece and it is connected to the barrel. So now, holding just the barrel (with mouthpiece attached) in your right hand, reed facing you, place the thumbnail of your left-hand halfway between the tip of the reed and the top of the ligature.

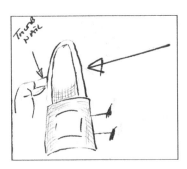

Thumbnail

With just the 'skin' of the lip over the teeth, slide the mouthpiece in until your thumb is against your chin.

Remove your thumb. Place your teeth on top of the mouthpiece. Relax your top lip. Adjust and adapt the positioning slightly until it feels comfortable. The angle between the mouthpiece and the chin needs to be somewhere between 40 to 45 degrees.

Draw your lips back as if you were tightening a washing line from either end.

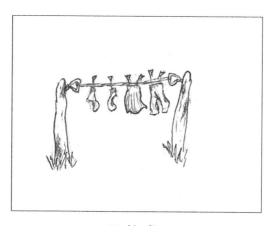

Washing line

Now, breathe heavily through your Clarinet as if breathing steam on a window. This is the *correct breathing*.

Steam on window

Blowing through the Clarinet as if blowing out a candle results in puffed out cheeks. This is *incorrect breathing*.

Blowing out Candles

Check in a mirror that your cheeks are not puffed out. Done correctly, there should be slight cheek dimples in your cheeks. Puffed-out cheeks result in bunching of the bottom lip.

The bottom lip muscles control the flexibility of the reed, so it is important they can work effectively.

The shape of the cavity inside your mouth (which makes up your sounding box) will also be slightly altered, affecting the sound you produce.

5

DIAPHRAGM BREATHING

ELEPHANTS AND BALLOONS

Make the most of your air. The diaphragm is like an elasticated rubber sheet resting between the rib cage and stomach. Used well, you can take in more air and control how you let it out.

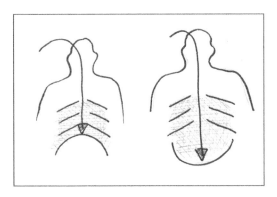

Less air, less control. More air, more control

How does it feel?

Place your palm in front of your face.

Blow onto your palm and the air will feel cold. You are not using the diaphragm effectively. WRONG.

Breathe onto palm and the air will feel warm. You are now using the diaphragm more effectively. RIGHT.

Now, place a hand on your stomach, just above your belly button and take in three short sniffs in close succession. You will feel your stomach puff up like a balloon.

Exercises to get started

Stand erect but relaxed with arms hanging by sides.

Imagine you are carrying a *heavy suitcase* in each hand – keep your back straight.

Suitcase

Feel the weight on each shoulder – imagine an *elephant sitting on each shoulder.*

Elephant

Now, place your hand back on your stomach, remember as before - just above your belly button.

Make three short sniffs in close succession again – remember the feeling of the stomach puffing up like a balloon.

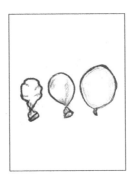

Balloon

Relax, and let the air out. Repeat a few times.

Now try continuing the sniffs until your stomach feels fully stretched and full of air. Relax and let the air out. Repeat a few times.

Now open your mouth and LET the air into the stomach in one long swoop (stomach extends out). LET the air out (stomach relaxes back). Keep elephants on shoulders and repeat a few times.

(Just an aside here - the word 'let' is more useful than 'breathe' in this exercise. The word 'breathe' usually triggers automatic reverting to default breathing habits. Interestingly, if you were to lie on the floor, you would find that your stomach fills out when you breathe in, and relaxes as you breathe out).

Now pick up the Clarinet and take a long swoop of air into the diaphragm, and breathe out through the Clarinet on a bottom G.

Make sure that the elephants stay on your shoulders. *Check in the mirror. Your shoulders should not move.*

Test it out

Check how long your bottom G note lasts. You can do the breathing exercise (elephants and suitcases) anywhere and any time. The more you exercise, the longer your bottom G will last and the more control you will have over your Clarinet sound.

Caution:

If you feel light-headed, just take a break and come back to the exercise later.

6

POSTURE
TREE ROOTS

Keep your shoulders relaxed and remember the elephants on your shoulders.

Keep your elbows slightly away from your sides.

Keep the end of the Clarinet held up slightly. An approximate 40-45 degree angle to the body (the same as the angle between the mouthpiece and the chin). This stance will give you good arm and finger flexibility and optimise your control of the instrument. The sound will also project well.

Keep your legs comfortably straight and feet planted slightly apart. If you are securely attached to the floor, you will feel sturdy and grounded - more in control of yourself and your instrument.

Sturdy tree rooted in ground

Whatever situation you may be playing in, you will feel relaxed, less likely to suffer from nerves or anxiety, and will look more professional.

CONTROLLING TONE
TUBES OF SOUND

Everyone has their own Clarinet sound – this is your Clarinet voice. There are so many wonderful Clarinet players out there - past and present, Klezmer, Jazz, Classical, Rock etc – all so different. Personality shines through, too. The more players you can listen to, the more ideas you will bring to your own playing. You will sub-consciously select the sound you want to make.

The **very best** way to improve your sound is to spend time playing long notes.

Choose a favourite low note. Take in air using your diaphragm. Breathe through your Clarinet to make a long steady note. Visualise this as a solid tube of sound.

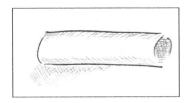

A solid tube of sound

Keep it level - no wavering.

Choose a higher note and repeat.

Choose a lower note and repeat.

As you become a more adept Clarinettist, you can switch between higher and lower notes across the registers.

The more time you spend on long notes, the better your sound will be.

If you do this daily, you may think your note tubes are wavering more than before, or your sound is not improving. This is perfectly normal. Don't be disheartened. You are only becoming more aware and perceptive, which is the surest way to success.

You cannot help but improve by spending time on this activity.

OPEN NOTES

BALANCING THE WEAKER NOTES - THE CHERRY IN THE
MOUTH.

Open notes

G, G#, A, B♭

These are all called 'open notes' because many of the
holes are uncovered. As you take your fingers off the
holes, in effect you are making the instrument
shorter and shorter. The sound can become thinner
and less easy to control. These notes can sound weak
in contrast to other notes and are more difficult to
keep in tune.

Remedy:

Firstly, use a little more air. Now imagine a cathedral – large and spacious.

Cathedral

Keep this visual image. You can make a bigger resonating space inside your mouth by opening out the throat slightly, and lowering the back of the tongue. Imagine placing a cherry on the back of your tongue while you play these open notes. (It should feel similar to stifling a yawn).

Cherry on back of tongue

Try playing notes in octaves, listening and adapting the air and tongue position to balance and match the sound. Remember to support well from the diaphragm:

Rich low 6-finger **G** - Yawning open **G**

Rich low 5-finger **A** - Yawning open **A**

Rich low 4-finger **B♭** - Yawning open **B♭**

NB

Playing can often sound 'lumpy', even if the fingers are fluent, simply because the sound isn't balanced across the registers.

9

POSITION OF FINGERS ON THE HOLES
FROG PADS AND HONEY POTS

The holes on the Clarinet are large. It is important they are covered completely so no air escapes from the tone holes. Squeaking in the upper register is often caused by slight air leaks where one or more of the tone holes are not fully covered by the fingers.

Keep the fingers floppy and relaxed – as if drumming the fingers on a table top.

Drumming

Keep a curved hand position – imagine you are gently holding an avocado in each hand.

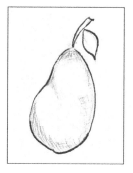

Ripe avocado

Ensure the pads of the fingers are covering the holes. Visualise a frog's finger pads.

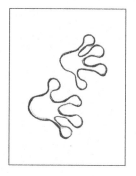

Frog's finger pads

You can test out whether your fingers are covering effectively in this way:

1. Gently but firmly cover the tone holes of the lower joint with the fingers of the right hand. Keep the left thumb on the thumb hole of the upper joint.

2. Gently plop the index finger of the left hand up and down. Listen very closely. You should hear a very satisfying 'plopping' sound.

3. Keep the index finger down. Now flop the second finger up and down....plop..plop..plop. Now the third finger...plop...plop...plop.

4. Now keep the upper joint holes covered with the thumb and fingers of the left hand. Plop the index finger of the right hand (there will be a slight key rattle with this one), plop the second finger, and then the third.

Pot of honey pouring out

5. Imagine you have poured a pot of honey down the Clarinet. <u>Do not actually do this!</u> When you are covering the holes, imagine you are preventing honey from escaping from behind your fingers, but do not squeeze. Remember to keep that lovely firm, yet relaxed finger position.

10

FINGER STRETCHING

AND MOORHEN

Notes can sound muffled or they squeak if the fingers do not fully cover the holes. Getting the fingers to move as you want means keeping control over them.

Try this for Co-ordination

First, hold up your left hand – palm facing away – as if saying 'Stop!' Keep your fingers closed – now stretch your fingers open – now closed.

Now try this:

1. Move just your little finger away from the other fingers and back.

2. Now, keeping little and ring fingers together, stretch them away from the other fingers, and back again.

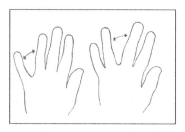

Little finger, ring finger stretch

3. Now move little, ring and middle fingers out and back.

4. Now move just the thumb out and back.

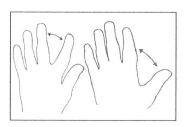

Index finger and thumb stretch

Repeat the whole process with the right hand.

Now try the whole process with both hands at the same time – you'll find co-ordination is easier.

Try this for greater stretch

Stretching fingers – visualise the stretched claws of a Moorhen and make your fingers do the same.

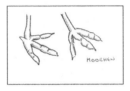

Moorhen toes

This exercise can be done under a tea-table when bored. Separate the little finger of your left hand from the rest of the hand by stretching it across your knee – try again with your little and ring finger together. Repeat with your right hand.

11

TWISTING ON THE PIVOTAL NOTE

FIRE ENGINE

The position of the left index finger on the A key is really important. Get the movement to the A key right, and smooth movement from lower register to higher register notes (going across the break) will be much, much, much easier further down the line.

Try this

Take the left hand off the Clarinet and hold it out as if you were going to shake hands with a friend. Instead of shaking hands, imagine you are twisting a door knob.

Twist the door knob

Notice how the wrist and forearm move as one.

Place your left index finger on F$^{\#}$. Play the F$^{\#}$ and, in the same breath, using a 'door handle' twisting action, move the index finger off F$^{\#}$ and catch the A key with the side of your index finger. Try to catch it just at the lower tip of the key – the key is slanted down to make this easy. Twist back to the F$^{\#}$ again.

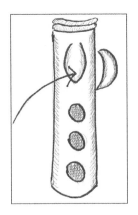

Tip of the A key

Repeat this action over and over again in one breath – sounding like a fire-engine.

Fire engine

Once you find this easy, move onto twisting to A from E, then D and lastly C.

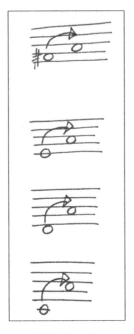

Twisting to A

Remember to make a *long tube of sound* whilst twisting – no bumps or blips.

12

LEFT-HAND THUMB POSITION
LEFT-HAND WRIST TWIST

The left-hand thumb and the left-hand wrist work together:

Wrist

Hold out your left arm and re-run the door knob twisting action **(Chapter 11)**.

Thumb

The left-hand thumb position is important, not only to cover the tone hole at the back, but also for flexibility and seamless movement between the lower and the higher registers on the Clarinet. Keep the thumb soft, floppy and relaxed — frog finger pads **(Chapter 9)** so the hole stays covered.

Check the angle between your thumb and the body of the Clarinet. Ideally it should be at a 40 to 45 degree angle, like the angle of chin to mouthpiece **(Chapter 4)** and angle of clarinet to body **(Chapter 6)**. (Interesting—those matching angles….the golden number?) When you do the testing exercise below, take this position as average and tweak slightly to get the optimum position for the length of your thumb.

Testing exercise:

Play a good rich sounding 6-finger bottom G – a long tube of sound, air supported from the diaphragm. Now move the little finger of the left hand slowly around a circuit of the *left-hand little finger keys* - G to E, G to F$^\#$, G to F - keep going round and round.

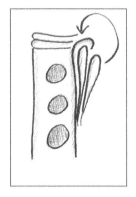

Circular movement round the keys

Make sure you keep the wrist relaxed and loose, allowing the door knob twisting action to happen as you reach for the furthest keys. If your thumb is in the correct position, you should be able to move freely across all the notes without uncovering any of the tone holes.

Once you can do this, try the same with the back register key on (top notes are less forgiving): D to B, D to C$^\#$, D to C.

13

RIGHT HAND THUMB POSITION
RIGHT-HAND WRIST TWIST

As with the left-hand thumb and left wrist, the right-hand thumb and the right-hand wrist work together:

Wrist

Take the right hand off the Clarinet and remind yourself of the door knob twist action **(Chapter 11),** but this time working with the right hand and forearm. Now place your right thumb under the clarinet thumb rest.

Thumb

The position of the right-hand thumb under the thumb rest is important. Too far forward and it will restrict the flexibility of movement of the right hand; too far back and it will feel insecure. Ideally it should be between the tip of the thumb and the thumb knuckle (where it bends).

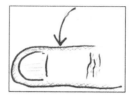

Between knuckle and end of thumb

When you do the testing exercise below, take this position as average and tweak slightly to get the optimum position for the length of your thumb.

Testing exercise:

Play a lovely, sonorous 6-finger bottom G – *a long tube of sound*. When happy, move the little finger of the right hand slowly around a circuit of the right-hand little finger keys G to E, G to F, G to G#, G to F#- keep going round and round.

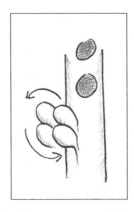

Circular movement round the keys

Make sure you keep the wrist relaxed and loose, allowing the door knob twisting action to happen as you reach for the furthest keys.

If your thumb is in the correct position, you should be able to move freely across all the notes without uncovering any of the tone holes.

Once you can do this, try the same with the back register key on, (remember, the top notes are less forgiving): D to B, D to C, D to $D^\#$, D to $C^\#$.

14

THE REGISTER KEY

A MERE TWITCH

Following on from the correct left-thumb position **(Chapter 12)**, the upper register notes can be reached by pressing just the very tip of the register key.

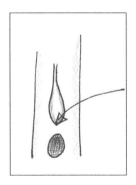

Tip of the register key

This is the tiniest, infinitesimal movement – little more than a controlled twitch. Watch your thumb do this and you will see how little the thumb needs to move before the key shifts to uncover the tone hole. The register key does not need to be pressed down fully to get the top notes. All you need to do is create a tiny air leak on the Clarinet and a top note will sound. Now try the exercise below and experiment with how little you need to move your thumb to get the upper register.

The Register Key Twitch exercise:

Play a rich bottom G – six fingers floppy on the Clarinet – *tube of sound*. Now just twitch the register key to get a top D and continue holding that top note.

Play a rich bottom A – five fingers floppy on the Clarinet – *tube of sound*. Now just twitch the register key to get a top E and continue holding that top note.

Continue working on from B^b, C and any other note in the lower register that takes your fancy.

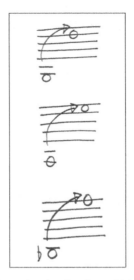

Tipping register key from low to high notes

N.B:

As you take more fingers off holes to create higher sounds you may have problems sustaining the notes. Check out the tips on Strong Top Notes (**Chapter 15**).

STRONG AND SECURE TOP NOTES

ANCHOR - BE BRAVE

A strong, rich and secure sound in the lower register is an excellent anchor on which to build top notes. Moving on from the Register Key twitch exercise **(Chapter 14)**, you should find that top D, E, F are easy to hold, but if the notes break or squeak as you go higher, then check out the points below:

Increased air pressure

Many people are scared of squeaking on the higher notes, and so they use less air. The reed needs to vibrate faster for the higher notes to sound. If you don't keep the pressure of air going through the Clarinet, the reed will stop vibrating and there will be no sound. Either that, or the reed will vibrate too slowly and you will just make a groaning sound.

Solution:

Visualise the *solid tube of sound* **(Chapter 7)** and use plenty of air support from the diaphragm. Don't slacken off.

Too much tension. Sometimes the top notes won't sound at all. If you feel tense about playing higher, it is easy to start biting. This presses the reed against the tip of the mouthpiece and closes up the gap – the reed becomes constricted and the air can't get through to make it vibrate.

Solution:

Try putting a tiny bit more mouthpiece in your mouth, just to open things up. When you feel more secure, just keep the pressure of air up but ease the mouthpiece out again to a comfortable position that allows the top sounds to come through. You can make a rounder tone by imagining the cherry sitting on the back of your tongue **(Chapter 8)**.

Not enough tension.

To keep the reed vibrating at a faster pitch, the bottom lip needs to be pulled taut.

Solution:

Imagine your lips as a washing line pulled taut at either end (**Chapter 4**). Keep the tube of sound solid, supporting it from the diaphragm.

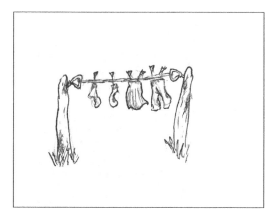

Washing line

The reed is too soft.

The thinner the reed, the more flexible it is. This is not always a good thing. As you use more tension in the lower lip, a reed that is too thin will be pushed too close to the mouthpiece tip and restrict the air flow. Reeds also become thinner with age (acid in the saliva eats through the wood), so consider how long ago you changed your reed.

Lemon. Acid!

Solution:

Put on a new reed. If you can't do this until later, then a good quick fix to keep you going in situ is to adjust the reed higher so that it is in line with the top of the mouthpiece with no 'thumb nail' of black showing. This really is just a short-term fix, until you have an opportunity to pop a new one on.

If the problem persists, then you may be ready to move onto a stronger reed. The 1.5 reed is a thin and easy reed to start playing on. The likelihood is that your lip muscles are strengthening and developing.

As you increase the tension in the lower lip for the higher register, the thinner reed will be pushing too close to the mouthpiece tip and restricting the air. If you are on a strength 1.5, then move up to a 2. The higher the number, the thicker the reed. (**Chapter 22**) for more on reeds.

16

HAND CLOSE

RELIEVING TENSION - DRUMMING

Watch any professional player and their fingers seem hardly to move. The more you move your fingers, the more likely they are to go down in the wrong place – not covering holes – catching other keys (squeak!) – and you will not be able to play quickly.

Try the finger plopping exercise again (**Chapter 9**). Now start to squeeze all the fingers down on their holes. Then try moving the fingers of the left and right hand up and down. They will feel sluggish and slow and you will feel tension in your right and left forearm.

Now shake your left arm and then your right arm, and shake your left hand and then your right hand – roll your shoulders around.

Drum the fingers of your right hand, then left hand on a table.

Drumming

Do the finger plopping exercise again (**Chapter 9**).

Try the fire-engine exercise (**Chapter 11**).

Try the *Testing* exercise (**Chapter 12**).

Try the *Testing* exercise (**Chapter 13**).

How close are your fingers?

17

TONGUING

OWL SOUNDS

Tonguing is the technique of separating one note from the next with the tongue. Most beginners stop and start the note by blowing HOO HOO HOO, or opening and closing the throat, creating an OO OO OO sound.

Clarinet tonguing can be more challenging for some than others, depending on your tongue shape and the way you pronounce words, but it is worth working on. A correct tonguing technique will produce a clear beginning to each note and allow you to play more quickly in the long run.

Try this: (Whisper, no vocal chords):

- OO OO OO (throat opens and closes)

- THOO THOO THOO (tongue flicks between teeth)
- TOO TOO TOO (tip of tongue touches roof of mouth lightly)
- DOO DOO DOO (area just behind the tip of the tongue touches roof of mouth with a slightly heavier action)
- DOO DOO DOO, TOO TOO TOO or somewhere between the two will work for you.

Now try this:

Get a *solid tube of sound* going on a nice easy note. Now bring in the DOO/TOO action. The tongue acts like a tiny little hammer hitting the reed and separating the notes, chopping up that tube of sound into segments of tube – separate notes.

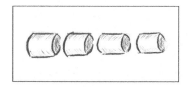

Chopped up tubes of sound

Every time the tongue hits the reed, it stops it vibrating. As long as you keep the tube of air going, the reed will vibrate again when the tongue moves away from the reed. The crucial thing is to keep that tube of air going as you tongue.

If this is all too tricky, try single notes - HOOD HOOD HOOD or HOOT HOOT HOOT. Next, move to continuous sounds: HOODOODOO or HOOTOOTOO.

Owl sounds

Once you can do this, progress to DOODOODOO or TOOTOOTOO (NB - you are now starting the process with your tongue on the reed, so you will feel the pressure of air behind the tongue before the sound is emitted).

Once this starts to come, it's a question of listening and experimenting to get the clearest sound, minimising the sound that the tongue makes hitting the reed. You will end up with more of the note sound, and less tonguing sound - it will begin to sound more subtle and 'clean'. If you visualise the chopped up tube of sound, the gaps between the bits of sound are getting smaller.

18
___

SCALES
WHY BOTHER?

Why play Scales?

Because scales are the quickest way to learn all the most common finger moves we use in playing music.

Why don't people like playing them?

Because most people get frustrated. They spend ages playing them over and over to get them right, and then when they come back to them later, they go wrong again.

Why does this happen?

Every time a scale goes wrong, your fingers are learning the wrong pattern. If you play the scale over and over, getting it wrong, then you are training your

64

fingers to play a wrong finger pattern – motor memory.

Playing a scale wrong is therefore actually worse than not playing a scale at all!

Why are wrong notes unsettling to hear?

Hearing a different sound to the one you are expecting can be an uncomfortable experience.

Solution

When learning a scale for the first time, play it so... so....slowly that you cannot possibly go wrong. It is best to read it from some kind of notation to start off with. Be sure to read the note and know what the fingering is for that note *before* your fingers move there. It is tempting to let the fingers take off and do their own thing.

If you do play a wrong note, correct it – go back to the beginning of the scale and play only as far as the offending note, but finish on the corrected note this time. *Stop*. Play from the beginning again.

Do this three times and you will have re-trained your fingers so that they get it right next time.

Each stair the same space from the last

When you feel more secure with your scale, be content to play slowly and steadily. Imagine an elderly person plodding upstairs. You can upgrade to a more youthful jog when you are feeling even more confident.

19

PRACTICE ROUTINE
WATCH TV

Little and often is best. You are likely to progress more quickly with just a few minutes each day than exhausting yourself with a three-hour session at the weekend.

Keep the Clarinet accessible - invest in a Clarinet stand. Keep the Clarinet out on a stand rather than packed away in a case. Playing a tricky bit of technique while the kettle's boiling, or a few scales while waiting for a phone call is a sure way to save time and move your playing on quickly.

Have a routine. Playing long notes is the best way to start. Get control of your breathing and embouchure. *Rich tubes of sound.*

Next, scales and finger exercises – get control of the fingers.

Then tricky sections of pieces (whilst the mind is still fresh).

Lastly, whatever you fancy.

Vary the tasks. If you are bored with long notes, just do a couple, then move onto something else. If you struggle with a scale or a tricky bit of music, don't keep going beyond the point of weariness or frustration – move on to playing something for fun.

Always try to bring in something utterly new – try new ways of doing things: new finger exercises and routines, new music.

Keep inspired and fresh - Listen to other players and recordings, keep yourself open to new ideas.

Have specific targets to work towards – a "performance" can be as understated as playing a tune to a friend. Aspirations to improve technique can be as humble as being able to play smoothly from one tricky note to another.

Take a break. If your concentration flags, do something entirely different – watch TV, go for a walk – whatever – and amazingly enough, when you come back later – you may well find the niggle you were struggling with has suddenly become easier.....your brain has been working on it while you were away from the Clarinet altogether!

TV

20

HOW TO PLAY TRICKY BITS
LOOKING AT THE WALL

Memorising is a valuable tool. By looking away from the music, you can really think about what your fingers are doing and train them quickly to do what you want.

Try this:

Circle the bit you can't play. If this is a whole line of notes, play slowly and work out which notes are the most difficult to move between. Narrow it down to the most challenging three notes, or maybe even just two. Play these notes very slowly from the music three times. Memorise these notes and play them again while looking at a blank wall.

Blank wall

You have now trained your fingers into the right finger pattern. Go back to looking at the music and add in *either* the previous note, *or* the note following, so you now have four notes. Repeat the process with these four notes, playing from the page three times and then from memory three times. Continue the process, adding in notes, one by one.

Messy blips - If you have tried this tactic, but things still sound messy, try this:

Take each pair of notes in the phrase and listen carefully as you move between them. Check your fingers are moving together. If they move up or down at different times, then you will hear an extra note in between. Work out which finger is moving up or down <u>last</u>. Work slowly so that you can make that sluggish finger to move up or down <u>first</u>.

Now play the whole phrase and get a tad angry with the sluggish note. It will come out correctly because you are paying it extra attention and therefore anticipating it in advance.

Repeating wrong notes - If you keep playing a wrong note in the same place, don't keep playing it wrong – you will be working the wrong fingering into your technique. Go slowly enough from the beginning of the phrase to get the offending note correct. Then repeat three times ending on the **correct** note. Remember – motor memory – training fingers to do what you want every time.

Keep a check on the state of your brain

This way of working is rewarding, but very intense, so there will come a point when you'll feel tired and things start to fall apart. Maybe change to a different type of practice, now.

Play through something easy you enjoy, or walk away and do something entirely different. Your brain will still be mulling over the niggly problem. When you come back to it next time, you should find, surprisingly, that the awkward section is a lot easier.

21

READING MUSIC FLUENTLY
EYE HOPPING

If you listen to a young child learning to read, they hesitate between each word:

The.......cat.....sat.......on.......the.......mat.

Big gaps.

If you listen to an adult reading the same sentence, the words blend together:

Thecatsatonthemat.

No gaps.

Try reading the very first sentence on this page – the one in bold italic. Now read it again, but this time read it out loud. When you say the word 'listen', notice which word your eyes are focussed upon... probably on the word 'young' or 'child'.

This is because we scan ahead with our eyes – and of course reading then becomes fluent. In the same way, *music* will sound more fluent if you can read ahead.

Eye hopping

TIP

Rather than resting your eyes on the longer notes when you play them, use the time to read ahead to the next note. You can use this strategy when you get to a rest or a breathing place or the end of a line.

Consciously make yourself do this, and eventually you will find yourself reading ahead on the shorter notes, too. You'll continue to develop until you find yourself scanning ahead many notes at a time as you play.

22

MOUTHPIECE, LIGATURE AND REED
KEEP IT SIMPLE

Mouthpiece

You may have a top-of-the-range Clarinet, but it will still be difficult to make a good sound if you have an inferior mouthpiece. By contrast, you can have just a basic student Clarinet and make a good sound if you have a good mouthpiece.

There are many many mouthpieces on the market to choose from with different characteristics but it is best to keep simple at the outset.

A **Yamaha 4C** is an excellent inexpensive starter mouthpiece. You can always upgrade when you have gained enough technical control to really notice the difference in tone, as well as the listening experience to know what sound you want to create.

Ligature

A standard metal ligature with screws at the front is fine – but beware, some cheap quality metal ones can keep sliding off the mouthpiece, dislodging the reed. Be sure your ligature will hold in place as you tighten the screws. The fabric or leather type with the screw at the back is slightly easier to set up.

There are many on the market, and some clarinettists believe the type of ligature you choose can make a significant difference to the sound you make. It is an individual thing and, as with the mouthpiece, it's best to keep your choices simple and functional until your playing has progressed further.

Reed

The lip muscles will be weaker and under-developed when you first start playing the clarinet, so you need a reed which is thin and will vibrate easily with little resistance.

Reeds come in different thicknesses, the lower the number, the thinner the reed. There are many brands on the market and costs vary, but a poor quality reed will never give you a good sound.

Rico reeds (orange box) work well for beginners. Strength **1.5** is a good starting place. As you venture into the upper register and your lip muscles firm up, you can then progress up to a **2** strength.

Royal reeds (blue box) are also manufactured by Rico. They are slightly more expensive, but better quality. As your playing progresses you will appreciate the difference.

Once you have gained control of the upper register, keep assessing the sound you make. If you wish, you can then experiment with a harder reed, but take your time. It does not necessarily follow that the more experienced the player, the harder the reed. There are many professionals who find they can get the flexibility, resonance and roundness of tone they need on a softer reed.

Comfort and physicality play a part, too. As with ligature and mouthpiece, reed choice is very much a personal preference. These are all aspects to consider further down the line as you tweak your 'unique Clarinet voice'.

23

ACCESSORIES
BE PRUDENT

Think about this:

As with any new hobby, there are so many accessories out there to tempt you. Best not over-spend until you have been playing a while and know what you will really need. However, generally speaking, it's better to spend rather more for a good quality product to ensure it will do the job properly.

Useful accessories that really make a difference:

Clarinet Cleaner/swab: essential for cleaning – get a good quality absorbent one - not the felt variety.

Mouthpiece sterilizer: prevents germs collecting in the mouthpiece.

Cork grease: essential for keeping joints lubricated so they don't stick.

Bore oil: **Only** if you have a wooden Clarinet. Prevents the wood drying out and splitting.

Mouthpiece patch: rubber pad that sticks to the mouthpiece – eases vibration on teeth and makes playing more comfortable – thicker variety is best.

Thumb rest cushion: slides onto a metal thumb rest at the back of the Clarinet and saves you from suffering a sore thumb – the soft rubber type is more effective than the hard.

Clarinet sling: takes the strain off the right hand – less weight on the thumb – eases repetitive strain. Most types hook into the hole on the metal thumb rest. If there is no hole on your thumb rest, make sure the sling you buy comes with a slotted leather strip so that it will still attach.

Clarinet stand: keep the Clarinet on a stand and you'll pick it up and play more regularly. There is a collapsible design that stores in the bell.

Music stand: better than straining your neck to read at an angle – it will improve your playing position. The collapsible type is great for getting out and about and playing with other musicians.

24

CLEANING AND MAINTENANCE
CIGARETTE PAPERS - HOW TO KEEP YOUR CLARINET
HEALTHY.

Cleaning your Clarinet:

Use a good quality Clarinet swab – avoid the cheap felt strip variety – it won't absorb moisture. Take the Clarinet apart, pull the swab through each section including the mouthpiece, and dry off the reed.

Cleaning mouthpiece:

Fill a sink with **cold** water (hot water will discolour the mouthpiece), and a tiny drop of washing-up liquid. Hold by the cork (do not immerse the cork), and gently clean with a soft toothbrush. Rinse with cold water and dry. Spray the mouthpiece with (mouthpiece) steriliser afterwards.

Stiff Joints:

Keep the corks lubricated and it will be easier to put your Clarinet together. If the corks get dry, then the keys can bend with forcing. Just dab some grease on the cork and work it in with your finger. Be careful to wash your hands afterwards so the cork grease doesn't collect in the tone holes when you play.

Sticky Pads:

Cigarette papers: place one sheet between the pad and the hole it covers. Press gently down on the metal cup holding the pad while drawing the cigarette paper out. This cleans the sticky residue off the pad.

NB - two points. Make sure the pad is dry before you do this (see next point below). Avoid eating or drinking before playing. No sticky breath = cleaner pads.

Bubbling Sounds:

Look for a hole that is wet. Open the key to uncover the hole. While the hole is uncovered, blow a fast jet of air between the open hole and the body of the clarinet to get rid of excess moisture.

Place a sheet of cigarette paper between the pad and the hole it covers. Very gently, press down on the metal key. Open the key and move to a fresh, dry section of paper and press down again. Keep repeating until the paper has absorbed all the water and comes out dry.

Bore Oil – (wooden clarinets only). Use very sparingly. Put a few drops on your Clarinet swab every three or four months and just continue to clean with the swab as usual. The oil works into the wood and helps to prevent the wood drying out and splitting.

25

SQUEAKS
A SUBSTANTIAL LIST!

With experience you get to recognise the different kind of squeaks.

Squeak!

Reed broken - never adjust the reed by pushing the tip/beware of catching it on clothing.

Reed worn out – if you've had it on for more than two weeks try changing **(Chapter 15- acid)**.

Reed too soft – if you've been playing on the same strength reed for a while you may need to upgrade to a higher strength, ie: thicker reed **(Chapter 22)**.

Reed too dry – take it off and give it a suck.

Reed in wrong position – check it is in line and that there is a finger nail of black at the top **(Chapter 2)**.

Reed warped – check the tip. If it's wrinkled, take off and suck, then place it on a clean surface. Press the sloped area down with your thumb fairly firmly, and draw the reed back slowly from under your finger (you may need to do this a few times) - this will iron out any warping.

Mouth in wrong position – check skin of lip **(Chapter 4)**.

Cheeks puffing – check in mirror – steamy window breath, not candle blow, washing line tension **(Chapter 4)**.

Too much mouthpiece – edge the mouthpiece out a bit **(Chapters 2 and 15)**.

Fingers not covering holes – check finger plopping action and remember to keep fingers relaxed. Check fingers are stretching enough – moorhen toes (**Chapters 9 and 10**).

Fingers catching keys –check left and/or right index fingers are not catching the clarinet side keys .

Check curved hand position – avocado shape (**Chapter 9**).

Finger tension – relax – put the clarinet down and shake your hands, roll your shoulders around and shake your arms. Drumming fingers (**Chapter 16**).

Fault on the instrument – do a vacuum test: check the upper joint – holding only the upper joint, place left fingers on holes and thumb on back hole so all the holes are covered. Place the end of the Clarinet joint on the ball of the right hand so the tube is sealed, and suck hard on the remaining open end of the joint. A vacuum should build up. Pull the right hand away swiftly, and you should hear a satisfying popping sound.

Check the lower joint in the same way – holding just the lower joint, place your right-hand fingers on holes. Push down the right-hand low E key. Place the end of the Clarinet joint on the ball of the left hand etc and listen for the plopping sound.

If popping sounds don't happen, one or more key pads may not be covering the holes. Check with a repairer.

26

BACK PAGE

READING FROM THE END BACKWARDS

It is an odd fact that mistakes often happen towards the end of a piece of music. Here are some possible reasons why.

Typical practice habit

Most people start at the beginning (an obvious place to start). They go wrong, start again, go wrong, start again, etc, etc, etc.

The end of the piece rarely gets played

The beginning gets played many times, but the end of the piece rarely gets reached—so that section doesn't get played very often - it's not very familiar.

Concentration diminishes

Most people are more alert at the beginning of a task. We take for granted the simultaneous skill of reading music with the coordination involved in playing an instrument. This requires a huge amount of concentration.

Anxiety increases

As you venture into uncharted territory, the likelihood of going wrong is greater.

Solution:

Start your practice session with the end of the piece.

THE END

ABOUT THE AUTHOR

Louise graduated from the London College of Music with ALCM and LLCM and, after a further teaching qualification, began her first post as Woodwind teacher for North Devon LEA. Since her subsequent post as Clarinet and Saxophone tutor for Blundell's School, Louise's ongoing freelance work in Somerset has involved teaching people of all ages and performing with a variety of Classical, Jazz and Klezmer ensembles.

Her music projects have been many and varied. They include co-founding *The High Park Community Music School,* which enabled any child to play music; forming the adult band *Hoot* moving adults towards improvisation; and collaborating on *The Mosaic of Art and Vision,* workshops designed to teach children how to create art inspired by music.

Since gaining a B.Sc (Hons) in Psychology, Louise has been developing Wizwind, an innovative teaching method that fast-tracks music learning for people who *struggle to read* music, and liberates people who *struggle to play without* music.

During Covid, when restrictions have allowed, fellow musicians have trekked to rehearse in a large barn where Louise lives on a remote farm, warmed by a fire pit and overlooking fields of bemused cattle. The Lockdown Clarinettist was inspired by a realisation that not everyone is so lucky. Some insights from a friendly Clarinettist who has 'done her time in the cells' (as music students term it) might encourage and spur on the lonely blower at this challenging time.

Look out for further Wizwind inspirations. Coming your way soon!

Made in United States
North Haven, CT
20 November 2021

11333363R00055